AL-KARAJI

TENTH-CENTURY MATHEMATICIAN AND ENGINEER

PHYSICIANS, SCIENTISTS, AND MATHEMATICIANS
OF THE ISLAMIC WORLD™

AL-KARAJI

TENTH-CENTURY MATHEMATICIAN AND ENGINEER

SUSAN NICHOLS

ROSEN PUBLISHING®
New York

Published in 2017 by The Rosen Publishing Group, Inc.
29 East 21st Street, New York, NY 10010

First Edition

Library of Congress Cataloging-in-Publication Data

Names: Nichols, Susan, 1975– author.
Title: Al-Karaji : tenth-century mathematician and engineer / Susan Nichols.
Description: First edition. | New York : Rosen Publishing, 2017. | 2017 | Series: Physicians, scientists, and mathematicians of the Islamic world | Includes bibliographical references and index.
Identifiers: LCCN 2016000101 | ISBN 9781508171430 (library bound)
Subjects: LCSH: Karaji, Muhammad ibn al-Husayn, -approximately 1016—Juvenile literature. | Mathematicians—Arab countries—Biography—Juvenile literature. | Algebra—History—Juvenile literature. | Science—Arab countries—History—Juvenile literature.
Classification: LCC QA29.K326 N53 2017 | DDC 510.92—dc23
LC record available at http://lccn.loc.gov/2016000101

Manufactured in China

CONTENTS

INTRODUCTION....6

CHAPTER ONE
ORIGINS OF AL-KARAJI....10

CHAPTER TWO
BAGHDAD AND THE GOLDEN AGE OF ISLAM....28

CHAPTER THREE
CONTRIBUTIONS TO ALGEBRA....46

CHAPTER FOUR
AL-KARAJI'S CONTRIBUTIONS TO OTHER FIELDS....62

CHAPTER FIVE
AL-KARAJI'S LEGACY....82

TIMELINE....97

GLOSSARY....99

FOR MORE INFORMATION....102

FOR FURTHER READING....105

BIBLIOGRAPHY....108

INDEX....110

INTRODUCTION

The Holy Quran, the sacred text of the Islamic faith, outlines the main beliefs of the religion. *Quran* means "recitations," and it is expected that Muslims, those who practice Islam, should be able to read it. There is another text, the Hadith, which compiles the sayings of the prophet Muhammad, the founder of Islam. One of these sayings, "The ink of a scholar is more holy than the blood of a martyr," tells us a lot about what Muslims value.

From the earliest days of Islam's rise, the prophet Muhammad encouraged literacy and the expansion of knowledge. For example, he banned many terrible practices that had been common on the Arabian Peninsula, such as female infanticide and slavery. As Muhammad and his followers spread their faith across the Middle East, they made it clear what observant Muslims should do to please God. These decrees are known as the five pillars of Islam. First, and most important, is the *shahada*, which is the creed of the faith. Every Muslim should believe the simple creed, which is, "There is no god but God, and Muhammad is his Prophet." This affirms that Islam is a monotheistic religion—a religion that believes in one deity.

The other pillars are *salat* (praying to God five times a day), *sawm* (fasting during the month of Ramadan), *zakat* (donating to charity), and *hajj* (making the pilgrimage to the holy city of Mecca in Saudi Arabia). Good Muslims, according to the Quran and the Hadith, should also not eat pork or drink alcohol. And, in their worship, they should be careful to pray only to God himself ("Allah," in Arabic) and not to any false gods or idols. For this reason, Orthodox Muslims do not celebrate—in fact they do not allow—images of anything sacred or divine. That means Muslim artists, unlike Christian artists, did not attempt to depict God, Muhammad, or any of the heavenly angels in whom they believed. This is a major shift from Christianity, in which depictions of God abound. For example, upon entering a church or cathedral, one can see artistic representations of God, Jesus, Mary, angels, and prophets everywhere: the crucifix, in stained glass windows, and in iconography.

Every religious community builds sacred places in which to worship their deities. What could Muslim artists do to decorate their mosques, the sacred spaces in which they pray? A solution was found: they could inscribe the walls with words, instead of pictures. Verses from the Quran's 114 chapters (known as *suras*) soon were painted on walls, and their Islamic artists' artistic skills were applied to the shape and design of the letters. The focus on calligraphy, which became one of the most prized artistic forms in the Middle East, emphasized the importance of language in the Islamic faith.

Artists also focused on designing books, buildings, pottery, and other items in geometric patterns, such as circles. Circles, which have no beginning or end, were viewed as representations of God, whose power is endless. Because artists cannot represent God in human form, they tried to represent him in a spiritual form. Geometric patterns are important. Muslim artist Dana Awartani says, "Islamic art is predominately made up of patterns due to the absence of figurative images and icons to prevent the art being a form of worship." She adds, "The main thing I love and respect about them is, even though they are all so diverse, they still share a common law. The idea of symmetry, harmony and structure is always at its core."

In fact, Awartani is highlighting something that earlier Muslim artists understood—at the heart of beautiful art, there was mathematical structure and design. Muslims turned art into math, and math into art.

Furthermore, in Islam's early days, schooling was an essential part of the faith. Good Muslims should learn to read, initially so that they could read the Quran and be enlightened. Classrooms were set up right in the mosque or in buildings attached to the mosque. Therefore, learning and religion went hand in hand.

Islam soon spread from Spain to North Africa to India. Throughout its growth, it championed education as passionately as it championed faith. By the year 750 CE, driven by the quest for knowledge and information, Islam had reached its Golden Age, in the city of Baghdad.

CHAPTER ONE

ORIGINS OF AL-KARAJI

Abu Bakr ibn Muhammad ibn al-Husayn al-Karaji was born on April 13, 953 CE. Unfortunately, despite the many contributions he made to modern mathematics and engineering, very little is known of his life.

MYSTERY OF A NAME

Even his name is a bit of a mystery for historians: some translators call him al-Karaji, which means "a citizen of al-Karaj," a town in Persia. If it is accurate, then this indicates that he may have been Persian, not Arab. Some translations of his work refer to him, however, as al-Karakhi, which indicates that he may have been from Iraq, from the city of Karakh.

Does it matter where al-Karaji was born? In one sense, it does. Persians and Arabs are two different ethnic groups, although both predominantly practice the faith of Islam. Persians speak Farsi and are from the land that today is the country of Iran. Arabs, in contrast, are an ethnic group that came from the Arabian Peninsula and speak Arabic. When Persia was conquered by the Arabs, many Persians converted to Islam. There was generally some friction between Persians and Arabs, as Arabs considered themselves to be the true champions of the Islamic faith. However, before al-Karaji's birth, the Islamic world came to be ruled by the Abbasids, who opened the empire to Muslims from all ethnic groups.

There is another element to al-Karaji's name. In some sources, one of his names is listed as al-Hasib. However, in Arabic, *hasib* means "one who calculates," or mathematician. Therefore, it is likely that this is simply a title used for al-Karaji during his career, rather than a family name.

Some scholars point out that, despite the uncertainty of his name, what is known is that Muhammad al-Karaji lived most of his life in Baghdad. He served as a vizier, a high-ranking official, for the Abbasid government from 1010 to 1015, and he even established a school for algebra in Baghdad. It was here that he penned three important textbooks on mathematics and algebra: *Al-Fakhri fil-jabr wal-muqabala* (*Glorious on Algebra*), *Al-Badi fil-hisab* (*Wonderful on Calculation*), and *Al-Kafi fil-hisab* (*Sufficient on Calculation*).

Al-Karaji's books were written in the 1000s CE, and they were important works of the day, helping to expand the system of algebra, which had recently been developed by Islamic mathematicians. However, after the fall of the Islamic Empire, it seems that al-Karaji's works were unknown in the West.

The books were not translated until the 1800s, by two Western mathematicians. Franz Woepcke was born in Germany in 1826 and studied mathematics and the Arabic language as a student. He had a deep interest in the medieval Middle East and is described by historians as an Orientalist. This term means someone who

Muslims believe that the Holy Quran was dictated to the prophet Muhammad by the angel Gabriel and that, therefore, it was authored by God. Every good Muslim should be able to read the holy words, which means that, from its beginnings, Islam promoted and encouraged literacy.

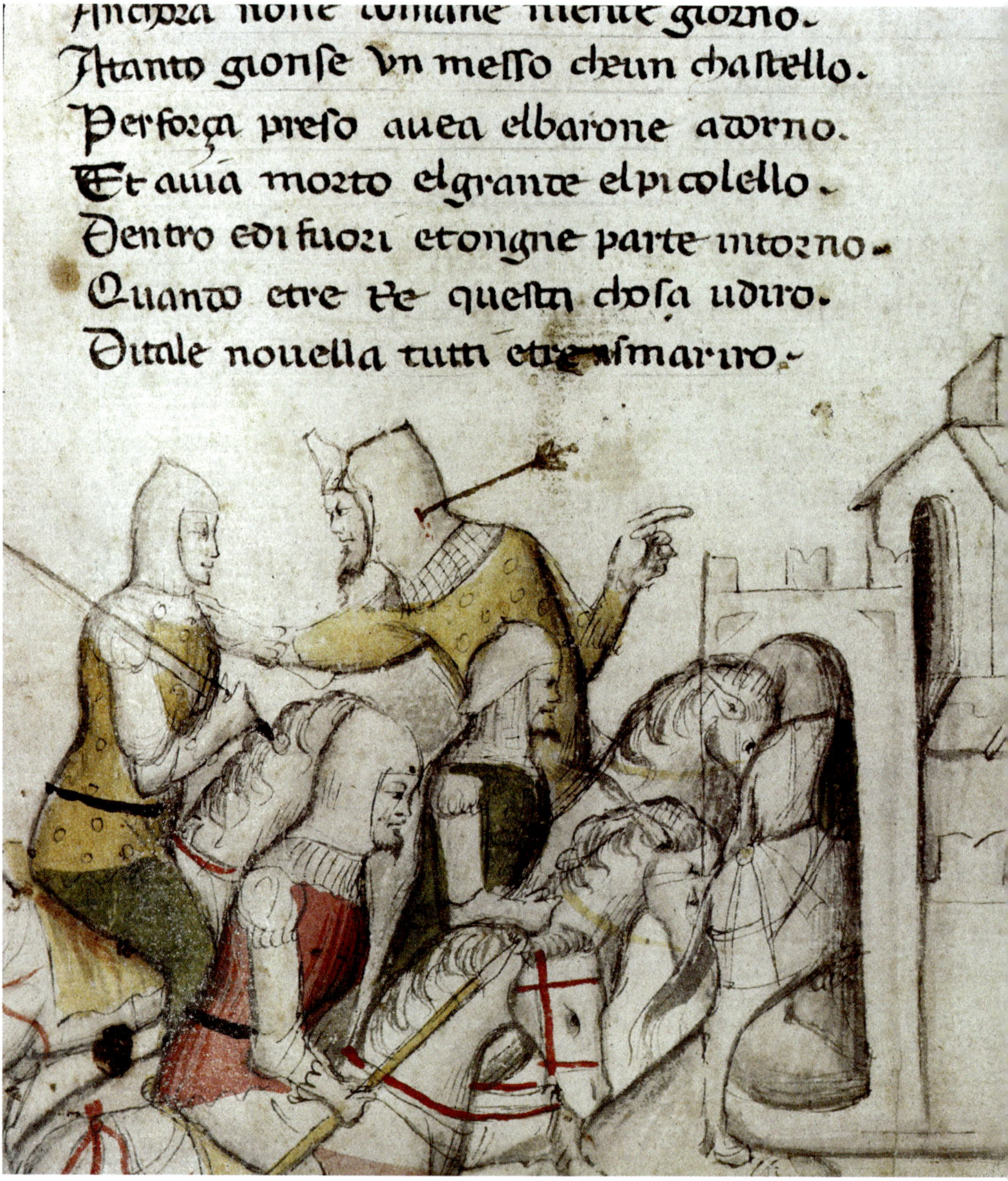

The Muslim Empire grew quickly and steadily. Before long, Muslims had conquered land across the Middle East, North Africa, and even Europe. Christian Europe launched its own response to the growing Muslim Empire: the Crusades, a series of battles waged against the armies of Islam.

is interested in "Oriental" thought, religion, culture, literature, art, and history.

"Oriental" used to refer to any part of the Middle East or Asia, and during the 1700s and 1800s, Europeans experienced an "Oriental" craze. The Crusades of the Middle Ages, a series of attacks by European armies on the Islamic Empire in the Middle East, were the first major interactions of East and West. There were many "crusades" over the course of four hundred years, all of which were attempts to defeat the Islamic Empire. It resulted in many deaths and the destruction of cities and towns, but there was also a cultural exchange that took place: returning Crusaders brought back discoveries from the Arabs to Europe. Among them were spices, silks, and hygienic and medical

WHAT'S IN A NAME?

Al-Karaji's full name may seem overwhelming to people unfamiliar with the Arabic language. It is important to remember that, like most cultures, the Arab culture seeks to designate a person's lineage in his name.

In Arabic, *abu* means "father of" and *ibn* means "son of." Therefore, al-Karaji's name, Muhammad Abu Bakr ibn Muhammad ibn al-Husayn al-Karaji, translates to Muhammad, father of Bakr, who is the son of Muhammad, who is the son of Husayn. In other words, in al-Karaji's name, we can learn the names of his father and grandfather, and even his son—a family tree in a name!

If this seems unusual, you may not realize that many non-Arabic names have similar systems. In Ireland, the prefixes *Mc-* and *O-* also mean "son of." For example, the name John O'Brian means "John, son of Brian," and the name Michael McDaniel means "Michael, son of Daniel." In French, the prefix "de la" or "du" has a similar meaning: Guy duJean means "Guy, son of John." In Scotland, Gregory MacArthur means "Gregory, son of Arthur." In some languages, such as Polish, the "son of" designation is used in a suffix, specifically *-ski*. For example, the name William Janowski means "William, son of John (Jan)."

In most languages, designating someone's lineage was vital, especially if it meant one could inherit land from his father or grandfather. He carried the name of his male ancestors as "proof" of his belonging to their family tree.

practices, as well as ideas about philosophy, mathematics, and science.

Europeans realized that the Islamic Empire had done the world a tremendous service; many ancient works of Greek, Roman, and Indian scholarship had been translated into Arabic and preserved. It was as if European scholars had stumbled upon a storehouse of information, just waiting to be translated and studied. There was a rush of young scholars who wanted to study Arabic so they could unlock the wealth of information that awaited them.

Franz Woepcke was one of these. Through his research, Woepcke discovered an algebra text by a writer he named Muhammad al-Karkhi. Woepcke was fluent in both German and French, and so he did his mathematical work in both languages. Woepcke translated a portion of al-Karaji's book *Al-Fakhri* into French in 1853. According to Sayyed Kowsar and Sayyedeh Kowsar, "This work encouraged historians to delve into books written in Arabic in search of scientific knowledge."

Another German scholar, Adolf Hochheim, also translated another one of al-Karaji's books. Hochheim was born in 1840 and published works on mathematics and geometry. In his translation of al-Karaji, Hochheim also refers to him as al-Karkhi. Hochheim translated al-Karaji's book *Sufficient on Calculation* in 1879.

It was not until 1933 that historian Giorgio Levi Della Vida argued that the medieval Muslim mathematician was more likely from Iran and named him al-Karaji. Levi Della Vida was an Italian Jewish scholar who was born in Venice in 1886. He was deeply interested in the religion and history of the Middle East and became the head of the department of Arabic language and literature at the Eastern University of Naples in 1914. During World War I, he served as an interpreter for the military and later accepted a post as a professor of Hebrew and Comparative Semitic Languages at the

One of the greatest dynasties in Muslim history was that of the Umayyads, who made their headquarters in Syria. They were succeeded by the Abbasids , who moved the capital to Baghdad, in modern-day Iraq.

University of Rome. His research and contributions to what was called "Oriental studies" were so important that there is an annual award given in his honor by the University of California at Los Angeles (UCLA). The winner is chosen by UCLA's Gustav E. von Grunebaum Center for Near Eastern Studies. According to UCLA, "The Giorgio Levi Della Vida Award is given to outstanding scholars whose work has significantly and lastingly advanced the study of Islamic civilization."

Most modern historians have agreed with Levi Della Vida that al-Karaji was originally Persian. However, no matter where he was born, Al-Karaji spent most of his life in Baghdad, which was under the Abbasids and a supportive environment for a scholar.

THE ORIGINS OF ISLAM

Islam is a religion with over one billion adherents worldwide. However, this belies its very humble origins in the deserts of the Arabian Peninsula.

Muhammad was born in the city of Mecca. A member of the large Quraysh tribe, he was orphaned as a child and worked as a trader, traveling across the Middle East. However, he was also a meditative and reflective man who spent time alone, thinking, on

Mount Hira. One day, in the year 610 CE, he had a vision of the angel Gabriel, who commanded him to recite. Muhammad obeyed, and he began to recite the words that would become the Quran. These visions came to him many times over the years. Muslims believe that Islam has always existed and that God chose to reveal his message to mankind in stages to various prophets, including the prophets of Judaism and Christianity. However, Muslims believe that Muhammad was the final prophet, to whom God's message was dictated in completion.

Muhammad began preaching the message of God and slowly winning converts, which made the powerful inhabitants of Mecca nervous. In 622, Muhammad and his small band of followers fled Mecca for Medina in a historical act known as the Hejirah. In Medina, they officially established the Islamic faith and that year, 622, marks the first year of the Islamic calendar.

Islam spread rapidly as a religion, winning many converts because of its simplicity. The essence of Islam is that one must recognize that there is one god, Allah, and submit to his will in everything. There were no layers of lesser deities or complicated rituals. It was also a religion that appealed to rich and poor, young and old, because it emphasized that one needed

Muslims believe that the angel Gabriel visited Muhammad one day, while he was meditating, and began reciting to him the words that would eventually be collected in the Quran. Finding a depiction is unusual, since Muslims are prohibited from representing the prophet Muhammad in picture form.

faith and moral behavior in order to do good, not money. Within ten years, Muhammad was able to return to Mecca with a large army and conquer it, establishing it as the center of Islam.

BEFORE BAGHDAD: THE RASHIDUN AND THE UMAYYADS

When the prophet Muhammad died in 632 CE in Medina, Saudi Arabia, his followers were left without a leader. The Prophet did not have a son, and so there was a debate about who would lead the Muslim people.

What happened next changed the course of Islamic history. It was agreed

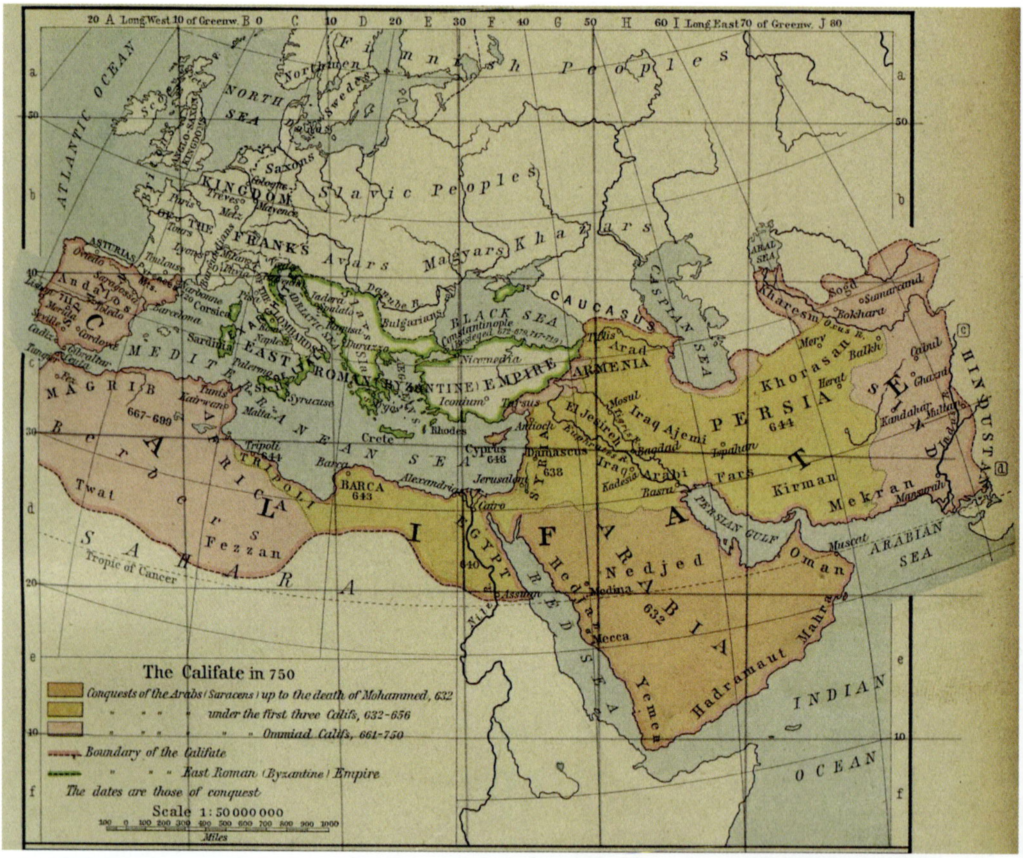

The Islamic Empire stretched across thousands of miles. It reached as far west as Europe, across North Africa, and as far east as Asia.

that Muhammad's father-in-law, Abu Bakr, was closest to him and would become the caliph. Abu Bakr was also a member of the same tribe as the Prophet, the Quraysh tribe.

In Arabic, *caliph* means "successor," and so Muhammad's successor would govern his people based on his closeness to the Prophet. Abu Bakr's caliphate was a successful one, and the Muslim tribe expanded into an emerging empire. The next three caliphs were also chosen because of their familial closeness to the Prophet: Umar, Uthman, and Ali. They were referred to as the Rashidun, or the "Rightful" caliphs.

However, even though the empire was growing (the Muslims seized territory in North Africa, Syria, and Jordan), the caliphates began to falter. Uthman was the third of the Rashidun, but he was not a member of the Quraysh tribe. He was born into a rival clan, the Umayyad tribe, but he was a wealthy man who had converted to Islam and who had married one of the Prophet's daughters. In 656 CE, he was assassinated in his home by rebels, and a major dispute broke out regarding who should succeed him.

Ali, another son-in-law of the prophet Muhammad, was chosen, but his selection was contested. A civil war erupted, which lasted from 656 to 661. Ali, the fourth caliph, was assassinated, and the caliphate was seized by his rival, Muawiyah ibn Abi Sufyan, of the Umayyad tribe. The Qurayshi tribe had been ousted.

It is Muawiyah ibn Abi Sufyan, who was governor of Syria, who established the Umayyad caliphate, a period of rule over the Muslim Empire that lasted from 661 until 750 CE. The Umayyads were a powerful force. Their headquarters were in Damascus, Syria, and they maintained a mighty army. Under the Umayyad caliphs, the Muslims conquered Spain and parts of India and Asia. The Umayyads were fiercely pro-Arab, desirous of keeping authority in the hands of ethnic Arabs, despite the fact that their growing empire now included Muslims of many other ethnic groups, such as Berbers, Semites, Turks, Persians, and others. They also made Arabic the official language of the empire.

The Umayyads began to show weaknesses, both internally and externally. The *mawalis*, the Arabic word for the non-Arab Muslims, grew more and more dissatisfied with their standing in their empire. Also, the Umayyad's army attempted to cross into France from Spain but were defeated in 732 by Charles Martel at the Battle of Tours. This win by the Frankish forces against the Muslims was seen as a great victory of Christianity over Islam. The advance and progress of the Muslims had been watched for centuries by the Christian Europeans, and now it seemed that they had been able to stop the advance of Islam in the West. For the Umayyads, the defeat by Martel was irreversible. Within twenty years, the Umayyad dynasty had weakened and completely collapsed.

The Umayyads were succeeded by the Abbasid dynasty, which ruled the Muslim empire very differently.

This image depicts the halt of the Muslim Empire into Europe. Charles Martel, known as Charlemagne, became the great hero of Christendom because he defeated the Muslim army in 732.

CHAPTER TWO

BAGHDAD AND THE GOLDEN AGE OF ISLAM

The Abbasids traced their lineage to al-Abbas, an uncle of the prophet Muhammad, thus returning the caliphate to the Quraysh tribe. While the Umayyads ruled, the Abbasids, who had become the weaker tribe, retired to Persia, where they began building alliances. Now that the Umayyads were the weak ones, the Abbasids stormed in and seized control.

GIVEN BY GOD

The first of the Abbasid caliphs actually called for the destruction of the entire Umayyad tribe, even though some of its members escaped to Spain and other corners of the empire. He wanted the Abbasids to have a new start, unburdened by the past. There would be a new vision that would guide the new caliphate.

The Abbasids came to power with the help of the Shiite Muslims, a segment of Muslims who believed that the control of the caliphate rightly belonged to the murdered Caliph Ali (Shia stands for "shia Ali," or the party of Ali). The Abbasids enjoyed the support of the Shias, but once they had assumed the caliphate for themselves, they did not make the Shiite demands their priority.

The Umayyad capital had been Damascus, but the Abbasids knew that they would be safer if their headquarters were closer to Persia. According to *Saudi Aramco World* magazine, Caliph Jafar Abdallah al-Mansoor said, "We Abbasids are a recent dynasty. We have supplanted the Umayyads, but we cannot be safe in their Syrian capital, Damascus. We must move closer to the Persian source of our power."

Initially, the Abbasids settled in the city of Kufa, but in 762 CE, al-Mansoor announced plans to build a new city on the banks of the Tigris River. The area, ancient Mesopotamia, had been populated for millions of years because it was in the heart of the ancient Fertile Crescent. The Fertile Crescent is the strip of land between the Tigris and Euphrates Rivers, where archaeologists have proved humans built the first settlements.

The new city was intended to be, from the outset, the headquarters of the Abbasids, and therefore, it had to be grand. It was named Baghdad, or "Given by God," and it was truly a magnificent city. At one point,

PERSIANS AND ARABS

Many people today confuse the ethnic groups of Persians and Arabs. While both of these groups hail from the Middle East, and while both groups are predominantly Muslim, there are, in fact, some major differences between them.

Persians are people whose ancestors are from the ancient Persian Empire, or the area that is modern-day Iran. They speak Farsi as their predominant language. Arabs, on the other hand, are people whose ancestors originate from the Arabian Peninsula and modern-day Syria, Lebanon, Palestine, and parts of North Africa. Their main language is Arabic.

Farsi is a language that uses the Arabic alphabet. If you think this is confusing, think of how English and Spanish are two different languages, but both use the same alphabet. The same is true of Arabic and Farsi.

Persian culture is ancient, dating back to 550 BCE, and the Persian Empire was one of the most powerful empires in the world. It was conquered by the Muslims in 633 CE, and soon after that conquest, Farsi began to be written using the Arabic alphabet.

Both cultures have a rich history and a long legacy

of beautiful literature and art. Both societies are also very family oriented. While the main religion in both cultures is Islam, both groups also have small communities that practice other religions. For example, before Islam, the main religion in Persia was Zoroastrianism, one of the oldest monotheistic religions in the world. Zoroastrians worship the Supreme Lord, or Ahura Mazda. There are still small communities of Persian Zoroastrians to this day. Likewise, in the Arab nations of the Middle East, most people are Muslim, but there are small, strong communities of Christians and Jews as well.

it became the biggest city outside of China in the medieval world.

Given the Muslim penchant for symmetry, Baghdad was built in a circular pattern, with a mosque at the center. The city was surrounded by four walls, named Kufa, Basra, Khurasan, and Syria after cities in the Islamic Empire. They were given these names because of the direction in which each wall faced. There was

Baghdad was built on the banks of the Tigris River. It was between the Tigris and the Euphrates Rivers that human civilization first emerged.

a second wall that served as a second layer of protection, and then a moat wound around the perimeter of the city.

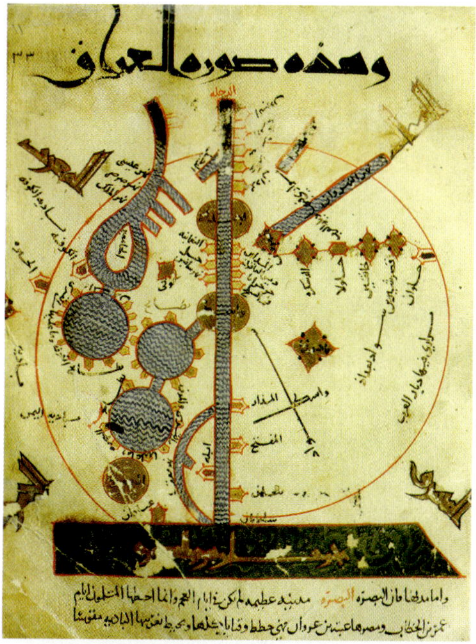

The city of Baghdad was built in the shape of a wheel, with the caliph's home, the Golden Gate Palace, at the hub.

The caliph apparently wanted the city to resemble a wheel, with streets and avenues emanating from the center like a wheel's spokes. At the center of the wheel, or the hub, stood the Golden Gate Palace, where the caliph lived and from where he ruled. Its main gate was layered with gold, which is why it earned its name. The top of the palace featured yet another circular symbol—a 130-foot-high (40-meter-high) dome, made of bright green stone.

Much of the literature and artwork that historians attribute to the Islamic Empire is actually inspired by the Abbasid reign in Baghdad. The Golden Gate Palace was like a glittering jewel, designed with ornate rooms, fountains, gold-encrusted pillars and walls, and other lush architectural features. The dining room could seat one thousand guests, and inhabitants did not need to be outside to enjoy a garden, as the palace's indoor gardens were exquisite.

THE HOUSE OF WISDOM

The Abbasids championed education and wisdom, taking the verses from the Hadith, the traditional sayings of the prophet Muhammad, about wisdom to heart. Some of these include the saying "He who treads the path in search of knowledge, Allah will make that path easy, leading to Paradise for him." Another saying claims, "A believer is never satiated with gainful knowledge; he goes acquiring it till his death and entry into Paradise."

In other words, for Muslims, learning begins with the Quran, but Muslims should always continue seeking knowledge. In Baghdad, the Abbasids built several institutions that promoted research and knowledge. There were many schools, hospitals, and research centers. One of the most famous of these was Bayt al-Hikmah, which means the House of Wisdom.

In the *Guardian* newspaper, the House of Wisdom was described as "an unrivalled centre for the study of humanities and for sciences, including mathematics, astronomy, medicine, chemistry, zoology and

The House of Wisdom assembled the greatest minds of Islam's Golden Age. These scholars translated classical Greek works and made their own achievements based on their Islamic ideology.

ISLAM AND EDUCATION

There are many verses in the Quran and sayings in the Hadith that support and encourage education and the quest for knowledge. The very first words of the Quran command Muslims "Iqra!" or "Read!" In fact, the word *quran* is a variation of *iqra*, so *Quran* means "readings" or "recitations."

In the Hadith, the recorded sayings of the prophet Muhammad, there is a scholarly approach to the ways in which statements were attributed to the Prophet. For example, rather than simply writing, "Muhammad said...", each saying is prefaced by a list of who heard Muhammad saying it. For example, a saying might be prefaced like this, "Mahmoud heard this, who told it to Ibrahim, who told it to Kareem," etc. In other words, Muhammad's sayings are recorded with citations—there is a list to back up that the saying is authentic. There was a tendency among early Muslims to document facts and to suppress myths and legends.

The Hadith attributes this statement on learning to Muhammad:

> If anyone travels on a road in search of knowledge, Allah will cause him to travel on one of the roads of Paradise. The angels will lower their wings

in their great pleasure with one who seeks knowledge, the inhabitants of the heavens and the Earth and the fish in the deep waters will ask forgiveness for the learned man. The superiority of the learned man over the devout is like that of the moon, on the night when it is full, over the rest of the stars. The learned are the heirs of the Prophets, and the Prophets leave neither dinar nor dirham, leaving only knowledge, and he who takes it takes an abundant portion.

Muhammad is also recorded as having said, "Every good Muslim should read the Quran." This statement does not discriminate according to gender. Muslim scholars have noted that Muhammad did not say "Muslim men," but "Muslims." Therefore, in the early days of Islam, women were permitted to attend schools and learn how to read and write. This is important to note because, in other parts of the world during the medieval era, women generally were not offered such privileges. In Europe, for example, the vast majority of women—except for a small percentage of wealthy noblewomen—were illiterate during this same time period.

Education for men and women was important to the Abbasids. This artwork by Yahya ben Mahmud al-Wasiti depicts students in a madrassa, or a school, being taught by Abu Zayd.

geography, as well as some more dubious subjects such as alchemy and astrology." The caliph sponsored scholars from across the Islamic Empire—from Spain to Persia to India—to come and conduct research in the House of Wisdom.

There were two major ways in which these scholars contributed to the knowledge storehouse. The first is that they began aggressively to translate works of scholarship from other regions of the empire into Arabic. Great works of philosophy from the Greeks, medical texts in Sanskrit, astrological works in Farsi—these were all translated into Arabic and studied by the Baghdad-based scholars. Those in the Islamic world did not begin reading and interpreting the scholarship of the ancient Greeks until the Abbasid dynasty. Once they did, these sources were accessible to Muslims.

The amount of information from around the world that the scholars were able to assemble was astounding. According to the *Guardian*, "Drawing on Persian, Indian and Greek texts—Aristotle, Plato, Hippocrates, Euclid, Pythagoras and others—the scholars accumulated the greatest collection of knowledge in the world, and built on it through their own discoveries." That is the second crucial contribution of the Abbasid-era scholars: they not only preserved scholarship, they expanded it and developed it further.

These accomplishments were made possible by two important features of the Abbasid era: first of all, Muslims championed literacy. It was crucial to Muslims that they be able to read the Quran directly—indeed, the very first words of the Quran are "Iqra!" which means "Read!" It is an order, and it continues, "Read! In the Name of your Lord, Who has created everything." Copies of the Quran were produced throughout the empire, and many mosques also functioned as schools. There are no official positions for priests or clergy in Islam, as it is assumed that every Muslim should be able to read the Quran and have a direct relationship with God. There are imams, holy men who have studied and learned a good deal about their faith and can serve the role of mentors or instructors in the Islamic religion.

This first accomplishment of the Muslim caliphate, the increase in literacy, was itself made possible by the way that the Abbasid-era scholars were able to produce paper. Paper was first produced in ancient Egypt; made from reeds that were pulped and flattened. It was easier to use than carving into stone tablets. However, it was not strong enough to last very long and difficult to use.

In China, around 100 BCE, a government official named Cai Lun began experimenting with making paper. He selected certain barks and plants, then mashed and pulped them. He then flattened them and allowed them to dry, which resulted in a relatively inexpensive and durable writing surface. His method became very popular in China, and because the exchange of information was highly prized by the Abbasids, the Muslim scholars of Baghdad were using this method almost one thousand years later.

The cheap cost and abundance of paper made scholarship more fruitful during the Abbasid era. Soon, paper mills were built throughout Baghdad, thus reducing the cost of paper production even further. Schools could function more efficiently, and scholars could work independently and easily on translations, problem solving, and research. They could produce books at a lower cost, which also helped promote literacy throughout the empire. Ideas that were born in the minds of scholars could be shared and spread to larger audiences from Europe to Asia. Furthermore, by writing these ideas down on durable paper, scholars could preserve their findings for later generations, reminding us of how far-sighted the Abbasids were in their scholarly contributions.

THE ROLE OF NON-ARAB MUSLIMS

The Abbasids valued the work and contributions of all Muslims, unlike the Umayyads, who prized their own Arab ethnic group. For the Abbasids, the family unit was formed by religion; a non-Arab Muslim could be a better companion than an Arab non-Muslim. The most important characteristic of a person was whether or not he worshipped Allah.

Therefore, the *mawalis* (non-Arab Muslims) flocked to Baghdad, where they knew their contributions would be welcomed. Mawali scholars were invited by the caliph's administration to live, study, and work in Baghdad.

Along with Arab scholars, non-Arab scholars benefited from the intense focus on science and mathematics in Baghdad. They

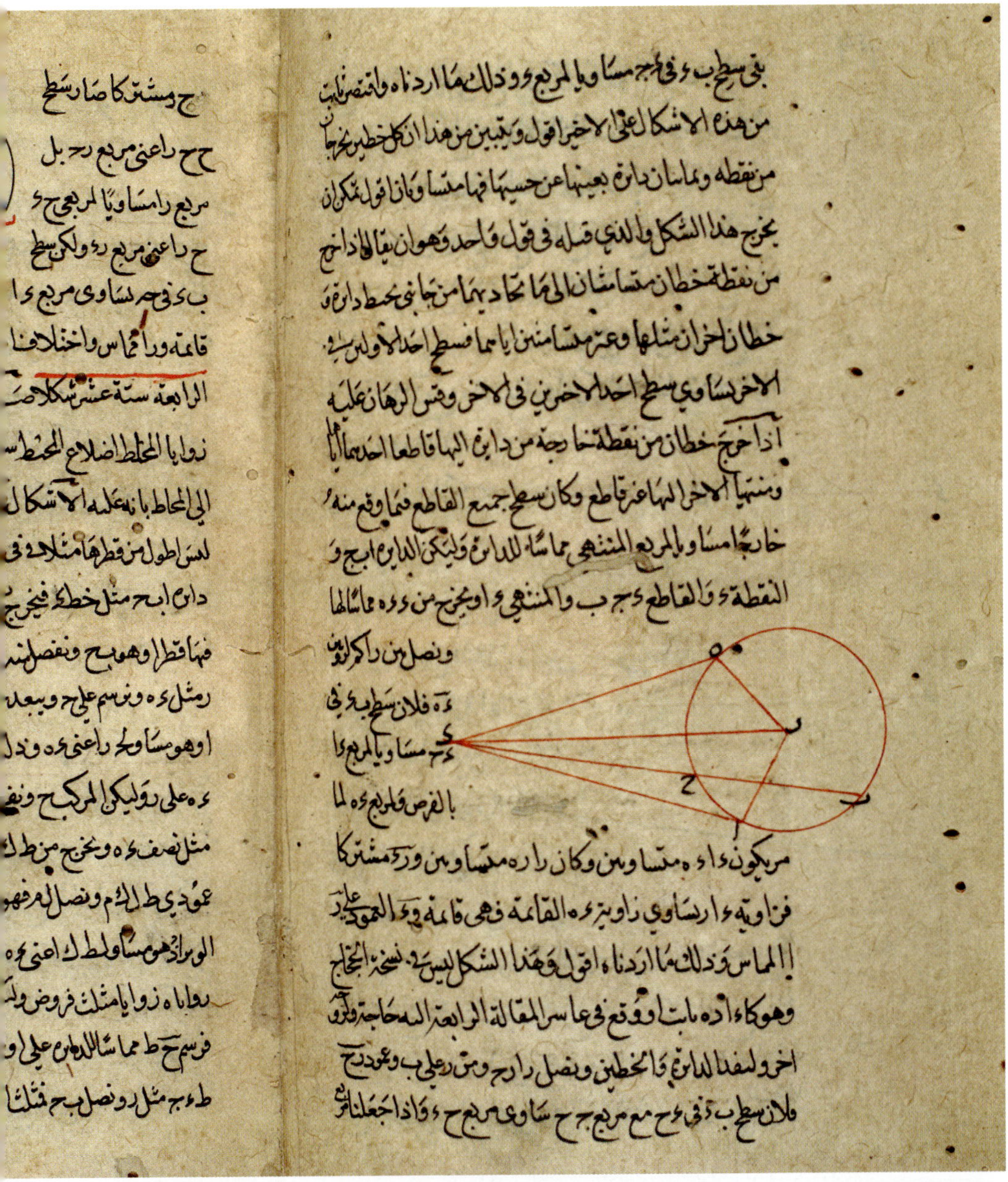

One of the most significant achievements of the Muslim Empire was its preservation of ancient Greek texts. This is an Arabic translation of Euclid's important work *Elements of Geometry*.

knew about Babylonian mathematics as well as scholarship from other parts of the world, but they were most deeply influenced by the Greeks and the Indians.

From the Greeks, the Muslims of the Abbasid caliphate translated Euclid's *Elements,* a massive work composed of thirteen different books. Euclid lived in Alexandria around 300 BCE and explained geometry and geometric algebra in his texts. He also defined many elements of number theory, such as the definition of a number as something composed of many units. He also defined prime and composite numbers.

Another important Greek work was the *Arithmetica* of Diophantus, a Greek mathematician who lived around 250 CE in Alexandria. His work was translated into Arabic by Abu al-Wafa and Qusta ibn Luqa, both Islamic mathematicians. The *Arithmetica* is a compilation of 260 problems that include both determinate equations (problems that have a solution) and indeterminate equations (problems that have more than one solution). Diophantus developed a way to solve indeterminate equations, which is known as Diophantine analysis. Diophantus is very important to the world of mathematics because of the way he argued for rational solutions to problems. The *Arithmetica* also contributed to the understanding of number theory: he is referred to frequently as the "father of algebra."

Indian mathematical works also were collected and translated. One of the most lasting contributions from Indian mathematicians was the development of the base-10 number system, in which the numbers used are called Arabic numerals today. However, they should more accurately be referred to as Indian numerals. They are a set of 10 symbols (1, 2, 3, 4, 5, 6, 7, 8, 9, and 0) that emerged in India in the sixth century CE and became popular because they were much easier to use than the cumbersome Roman notation system (I, II, III, IV, etc).

Furthermore, developing the zero was incredibly important because it did something previously unimagined: the symbol of zero was a way to represent "nothing." In other words, representing a lack of something was important in mathematics. Also, it allowed for place value to be used meaningfully. For example, 5 means five units, but 50 means fifty units. The inclusion of one zero represents the tens place in counting, while two zeros would represent the hundreds place, and so on.

One of the most important Muslim scholars, who would work with both Greek and Indian scholarship, was Muhammad ibn Musa al-Khwarizmi.

CHAPTER THREE

CONTRIBUTIONS TO ALGEBRA

Al-Khwarizmi was born in Persia in 780 CE. In 786 CE, six years after his birth, the renowned caliph Haroun al-Rashid ascended to the throne and ruled the Abbasid Empire until 809. Al-Rashid is one of the most famous figures to emerge from the Middle East, not just because of his leadership skills but also because of his charisma. He was known for dressing as a commoner and walking through the streets of Baghdad in such a disguise. He also had a great fascination with learning. He strengthened the Abbasids' commitment to scholarship, and this continued during the reign of his son, Caliph al-Mamun ibn Haroun.

It was al-Mamun who sponsored al-Khwarizmi to join the House of Wisdom. It was a historic invitation, as al-Khwarizmi would become one of the most influential mathematicians of all time. He was also a tremendous influence on al-Karaji.

Al-Khawarizmi is one of the most well-known mathematical scholars of the Muslim world. His work was a profound influence on al-Karaji.

The Abbasid era was a great one because of the foresight of its caliphs, who promoted learning and scholarly achievement. One of its great caliphs was al-Mamun, who is depicted here at the center.

Al-Khwarizmi eventually became the director of the House of Wisdom and oversaw many of the translation projects that were being undertaken. One of his most famous works was *Al-Kitab al-mukhtasar fi hisab al-jabr wal-muqabala* (*The Compendious Book on Calculation by Completion and Balancing*), which he dedicated to his patron and supporter, Caliph al-Mamun:

> That fondness for science, by which God has distinguished the Iman Al Mamun, the Commander of the faithful (besides the caliphate which He has vouchsafed unto him by lawful succession, in the robe of which He has adorned him), that affability and condescension which he shows to the learned, that promptitude with which he protects and supports them in the elucidation of obscurities and in the removal of the difficulties, has encouraged me to compose a short work.

In this "short work," which became long in terms of its influence, al-Khwarizmi explained the concepts of elementary algebra. In fact, the term "algebra" comes from *al-jabr*, in the book's title, which means the joining of separated parts. In fact, this is the modern definition of algebra, which is still central in mathematics today. Today, elementary algebra is the manipulation of symbols to represent the unknown. For example, elementary arithmetic would posit that $5 + 2 = 7$, but in algebra, one could use symbols to represent what is not yet known, such as $x + 2 = 7$.

Al-Khwarizmi did not invent this concept; indeed, Greek mathematicians had been using algebraic ideas in their development of geometry, but al-Khwarizmi was the first to use it in a clear, definable manner. His is a practical text, offering hundreds of problems and solutions, which advanced the study of algebra as a branch of mathematics separate from arithmetic and geometry.

A second book by al-Khwarizmi, translated as *Al-Khwarizmi Concerning the Hindu Art of Reckoning*, offered a useful study of Indian numerals, including the concept of zero. One of these was the work done by the Indian mathematician Brahmagupta on the number zero and how it should be handled: one plus zero equals one; one minus zero equals one; and one

WHY ALGEBRA MATTERS

Many middle and high school students express frustration with learning algebra, and they wonder why it is so important. Educators point out that algebra is a "gateway subject"—in other words, learning algebra and mastering it will allow a student to learn high-level math, such as geometry, trigonometry, and calculus.

What is algebra? Simply put, it is a way of understanding the relationships between numbers. For example, $4x + 5 = 17$ means that the terms on either side of the equal sign should be equal. Knowing this, we can figure out the unknown, which is designated as x. (The answer is $x = 3$.)

Having to figure out how numbers and terms are related allows students to apply critical thinking skills, rather than doing simple arithmetic, such as $2 + 3 = 5$. In her article "The Importance of Algebra for Everyone," Tricia Donovan writes, "Algebra is more than x's and y's. The notation expresses rules about how operations work; rules that students can reason out for themselves. This reasoning—about how numbers can be taken apart and put together under different operations—is the primary work of elementary students in algebra."

Al-Karaji's contributions to algebra opened it up as an independent field of mathematics. His successors continued to build on his work, as algebra developed into an essential tool for people in various professions, such as engineers, architects, and computer scientists. Humans have always sought to understand what they do not know, and algebra is simply one tool for expressing this mathematically.

multiplied by zero equals zero. Al-Khwarizmi built upon this concept of zero and on the number theory found in the works of Euclid. The Latin translation of this second book presented al-Khwarizmi's name as *Al-goritmi*, which evolved into the term "algorithm," which is a mathematical term that means a method or procedure for solving a problem.

Al-Khwarizmi was, like his patron, fascinated with the study of astronomy as well. His third major book was *Kitab surat al-ard* (*The Book of the Image of the Earth*). Scholars had long known that the earth was round and not flat, and in this book, Al-Khwarizmi presented solutions for calculating the circumference of the earth. He also contributed to

Evolution of Hindu-Arabic num

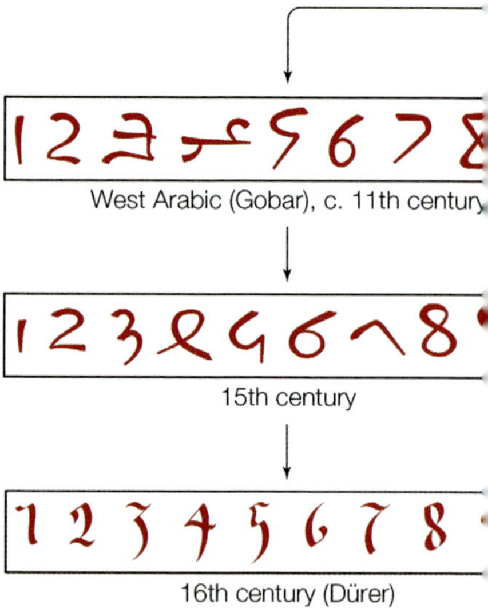

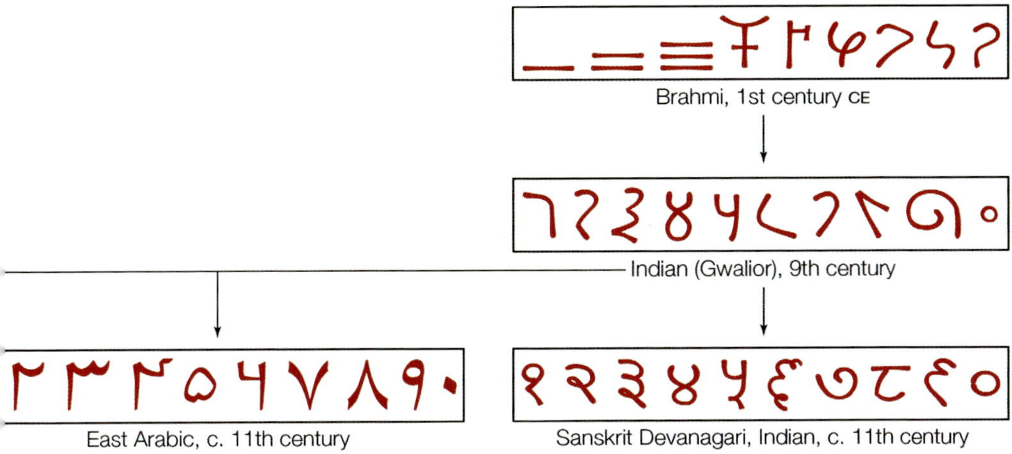

What are called Arabic numerals today really evolved from the numerals created by Hindu mathematicians. They revolutionized the way that scholars could compute and handle quantities.

methods for understanding what the earth looks like in terms of calculating the width of the Mediterranean Sea. Furthermore, he helped develop a world map that was as updated as possible.

INFLUENCE ON AL-KARAJI

Al-Khwarizmi died in 850 CE, one hundred years before the birth of Muhammad Abu Bakr ibn Muhammad ibn al-Husayn al-Karaji, who was born in 953 CE. Nevertheless, his influence upon al-Karaji is very deep and lasting.

Under al-Khwarizmi's directorship of the House of Wisdom, Baghdad had become a powerful center of learning, attracting the best minds and moving beyond translating important ideas to producing them. Al-Khwarizmi had also favored the mathematical contributions of Indian and Greek scholars, and al-Karaji did the same.

According to Jacques Sessiano in his article in *Encyclopaedia of the History of Science, Technology, and Medicine in Non-Western Cultures*, al-Karaji "combined tradition and novelty in his mathematical exposition." In other words, he relied on the scholarship of previous mathematicians, such as al-Khwarizmi and the Greek scholar Diophantus, but he also offered his own original solutions and ideas.

He studied mathematical expressions called monomials, binomials, and polynomials. A monomial contains one ("mono") term ("nomial"); this means it can have a positive number and a coefficient or a variable. An example of a monomial would be 3xy2. A polynomial is a mathematical expression meaning "many" ("poly") terms. A polynomial might look like this: 3xy2 – 1 + 2x. A binomial is a polynomial that contains exactly two ("bi") terms, such as 3xy2 – 1.

The first work that al-Karaji wrote was titled *Al-Fakhrifil al-jabr wal-muqabala* (*Glorious on Algebra*), which was dedicated to a vizier of Baghdad, Fakhr al-Mulk. It was described by Woepcke, who translated it, as "the most complete or rather the only theory of algebraic calculus among the Arabs known to us up to the present time," according to Roshedi Rashed in *Dictionary of Scientific Biography*. Al-Karaji studied the *Arithmetica* of Diophantus and applied some of the practical techniques pioneered by his predecessor al-Khwarizmi. For the Greeks, algebra was tied up with geometry, but al-Karaji was able to "separate algebraic operations from the geometric representations given to them by the Greeks," according to Tucker McElroy in *A to Z of Mathematicians*.

What this means is that al-Karaji was able to take the concept of algebra and apply arithmetical operations to it. This is vital to the development of modern algebra. Rashed explains, "This arithmetization of algebra was based both on algebra, as conceived by al-Khwarizmi and developed by Abu Kamil and many others, and on the translation of the *Arithmetica* of Diophantus." Rashed says that al-Karaji's work allowed for "a new departure in algebra." McElroy agrees that al-Karaji's "approach was completely new." It is important to note that many scholars agree that al-Karaji's work was original and groundbreaking because many others believed he was simply repeating ideas already articulated by al-Khwarizmi.

In *Glorious on Algebra*, al-Karaji offers a description of monomials, binomials, and the algebra of polynomials. He offers a method for adding, subtracting, and multiplying polynomials. In their biography *Abu Bekr ibn Muhammad ibn al-Husayn al_Karaji*, J. J. O'Connor and E. F. Robertson explain:

> What al-Karaji achieved in Al-Fakhri was first to define the monomials x, x^2, x^3, ... and $1/x$, $1/x^2$, $1/x^3$, . . . and to give rules for products of any two of these. So what he achieved here was defining

the product of these terms without any reference to geometry. In fact he almost gave the formula

$x^n x^m = x^{m+n}$ for all integers n and m

but he failed to make the definition $x^0 = 1$ so he fell just a little short.

Al-Karaji did not succeed in dividing polynomials thoroughly; he only divided polynomials by monomials. O'Connor and Robertson explain that al-Karaji then looked at "composite quantities," or sums of monomials. For these he gave rules for addition, subtraction, and multiplication but not for division in the general case, only giving rules for the division of a composite quantity by a monomial. He was able to give a rule for finding the square root of a composite quantity, which is not completely general since it required the coefficients to be positive, but it is still a remarkable achievement."

AL-BADI FIL-HISAB

His second book, *Al-Badi fil-hisab* (*Wonderful on Calculation*) is, according to Jacques Sessiano, "more original" than *Glorious on Algebra*. Al-Karaji reviews many of Euclid's ideas and then demonstrates ways to "calculate with square, cubic, and biquadratic roots with their sums." Al-Karaji adds a section that teaches the reader how to "extract the root of a polynomial in x," which, Sessiano explains, is the first known explanation of this procedure. It seems that, in *Wonderful on Calculation*, al-Karaji is not simply demonstrating previously known theorems and ideas; instead, he is using the work of Euclid and Diophantus and creating something new. Using their ideas, he is moving ahead to discover new possibilities with mathematics.

The importance of al-Karaji's work in *Wonderful on Calculation* became known in its influence on another Abbasid-era mathematician: Ibn Yahya al-Maghribi al-Samawal. His name, al-Maghribi, indicates that his family originated in al-Maghreb, which means northern Africa in Arabic. Indeed, al-Samawal's father was from Fez, Morocco, but he moved to Baghdad before his son was born. The family was Jewish, and many of them were very highly educated: al-Samawal had an uncle who was a doctor and his father was a religious scholar. Jews and Christians were welcome in the Abbasid court: indeed, many other famous scholars during this era were non-Muslims.

Al-Samawal would have been called, in today's terms, a child prodigy. He excelled in science and math to such an extent that he learned all his teachers in Baghdad could offer him when he was approximately thirteen years old. One source indicates that al-Samawal studied in al-Karaji's school, which seems to confirm that al-Karaji, while living in Baghdad, did indeed establish a center for mathematical education in the city. It must have remained open and enrolled students even after al-Karaji's death.

However, al-Samawal was not challenged academically in these formal educational environments. At that point, al-Samawal decided to embark on a course of self-study to push his learning even further. He absorbed himself in the writings and books of mathematicians and scientists of the era, including al-Karaji. Indeed, al-Karaji's works impressed the young scholar. According to al-Samawal, al-Karaji's contribution to algebra was "operating on unknowns using all the arithmetical tools, in the same way as the arithmetician operates on the known," say O'Connor and Robertson.

At the age of nineteen, al-Samawal wrote his own mathematics book, *Al-Bahir fil jabr* (*Brilliant on Algebra*). In this work, he improved on the ideas of al-Karaji. By discussing al-Karaji's work and where it falls short, and then demonstrating an improvement, al-Samawal was offering one of the first in-depth analyses of al-Karaji's work that survives to this date.

Specifically, al-Samawal noted that al-Karaji had come close to solving problems with irrational numbers; al-Samawal was able to solve them, building upon al-Karaji's ideas. In addition, al-Samawal describes al-Karaji's creation of what has come to be known as the binomial theorem, which does not survive in any of al-Karaji's work. Therefore, what we know of the binomial theorem and al-Karaji's contribution comes from al-Samawal's description. The binomial theorem in mathematics is a pattern that develops when you multiply a binomial (a mathematical equation with two terms) by itself many times over.

It was also al-Samawal who describes al-Karaji's work on what became known as Pascal's triangle. Al-Karaji was apparently the first to discover the number pattern within a triangle that is formed by arithmetical calculations. According to al-Samawal, as quoted in O'Connor and Robertson:

> Let us now recall a principle for knowing the necessary number of multiplications of these degrees by each other, for any number divided into two parts. Al-Karaji said that in order to succeed we must place "one" on a table and "one" below the first "one," move the first "one" into a second column, add the first "one" to the "one" below it. Thus we obtain "two," which we put below the transferred "one" and

It is believed that al-Karaji first described this concept in which a number in the triangle equals the sum of the two numbers above it. However, the credit went to French mathematician Blaise Pascal. It is known today as Pascal's Triangle.

> we place the second "one" below the "two." We have therefore "one," "two," and "one."

In other words, if one begins with "one," you put its factors below it, then you would see sums created. In this pattern, each number in the triangle is the sum of the two numbers above it. This was later dubbed Pascal's triangle, after Blaise Pascal, a French mathematician who lived in the seventeenth century, even though it is acknowledged that Pascal simply made the properties of the triangle known and developed it further. It had already been "discovered" by al-Karaji more than six hundred years prior to Pascal's birth.

CHAPTER FOUR

AL-KARAJI'S CONTRIBUTIONS TO OTHER FIELDS

Al-Karaji wrote a third known book. *Al-Kafi fil hisab* (*Sufficient on Calculation*) is more of a textbook written for civil servants. At one point in his career, al-Karaji was appointed to the position of a vizier within the Abbasid caliph's government. In this position, it was his duty to provide a handbook to others who were perhaps working on engineering or accounting tasks for the Baghdad civil administration. *Sufficient on Calculation* is a book meant to update civil servants on elementary algebra and geometry and other problems that they might encounter in their day-to-day activities.

GEOMETRY

As explained in the previous section, al-Karaji admired the work of Euclid, who defined many foundational elements of geometry. Al-Karaji added to these by defining, in his third book, *Sufficient on Calculation*, points, lines, surfaces, solids, and angles. He also explains to civil servants how to determine area and volume. This book, more than his other works, emphasized a practical use of calculation and the ways it could be used to solve problems. For example, he offers more than one solution and addresses the reader directly. In one section, according to Yvonne Samplonius, he explains one way to measure the volume of a sphere by making a wax model of the shape:

> You take a rectangular solid, made out of wax and with its three dimensions of equal length, and weigh it. Let its weight be 30 dirham. Now you make from this [material] a sphere, as perfect as possible, with the diameter equal to the dimension of the solid. The weight of this sphere is found to be a little less than 18 2/3. Hence, the diameter is raised to the third power and then 1/3 and 1/9 x 2/5 is subtracted. The difference between the two results is very small.

Again, al-Karaji is focused on solving real problems as efficiently and as accurately as possible. This was always his emphasis: what problems existed and what methods could be developed to help find an answer?

In Islam, worshipping images of God and important religious figures is considered blasphemy. Therefore, Muslims focused on decorating their holy places, like mosques, with the words of the Quran, in calligraphy, and in geometrical designs that celebrated symmetry.

RETIRING TO PERSIA

At some point in his career, after 1015, al-Karaji decided to leave Baghdad. The reasons are unknown, simply because historians do not have much information about his personal life. Did he leave because he was not satisfied in some way with life or with his work in Baghdad? We cannot know this, and there is no reason to suggest that the culture of Baghdad changed in any way. Indeed, from what history tells us, the Abbasid caliphs continued to be very supportive of academic scholarship and studies for years after al-Karaji's time at the House of Wisdom.

One source indicates that al-Karaji left Baghdad because his patron, Fakhr al-Mulk, was assassinated, but this is difficult to confirm. By 1015, al-Karaji would have been approximately sixty-two years old and perhaps ready to leave the busy city of Baghdad for a quieter life.

It is recorded that al-Karaji retired to the "mountainous country" of Persia, which may offer some confirmation that he was originally Persian. Perhaps he was simply returning to the region of the Islamic Empire in which he was born or from where his ancestors originated.

Established in approximately 30 BCE, Karaj is the fourth most populated city in Iran (modern-day

The Elburz Mountains in Iran are a popular skiing destination. When al-Karaji retired from his work and left Baghdad, he returned to this region in Persia, now called Iran.

Persia) today. It can indeed be described as "mountainous" because it is nestled in the lower hills of the Elburz Mountains, a range that separates the Caspian Sea from the rest of the country. The Elburz Mountains receive heavy snowfall in the winters and today they are a popular destination for Iranians who enjoy skiing. That same snow provides much of the needed water to much of the arid land in their shadow.

Therefore, it is likely that al-Karaji returned to the city of Karaj and lived the rest of his life in the shadow of the Elburz Mountains. However, he did not retire from his work in the least. In fact, these later years in Persia were spent being incredibly productive.

HIDDEN WATERS

One of the biggest problems in the medieval Abbasid Empire—a problem that remains today—is how to access water. The Middle East, which is a region that includes North Africa, the Arabian Peninsula, and modern-day Syria and Iran, is in a warm and dry climate.

This is a mountainous area that experiences frequent and repeated meteorological droughts. This has been the case for centuries. The ancient Persians struggled to find ways to access water because the region receives so little rainfall.

Scientists of the Abbasid era were interested in ways to maximize water usage. One method that has been used for centuries is extracting water, or pulling it, out of the ground. Al-Karaji contributed to this quest. He authored a book titled *Inbat al-miyah al-khafiya* (*The Extraction of Hidden Waters*). The book, which was only discovered in the 1970s, describes ways to detect underground water, access and retrieve it, and then transport it to locations where it is needed. In fact, it is possible that he coined the Arabic word for "extraction"—*inbat*—in the title of his book. He may have created it as a variation of the Arabic word *istenbat*, which

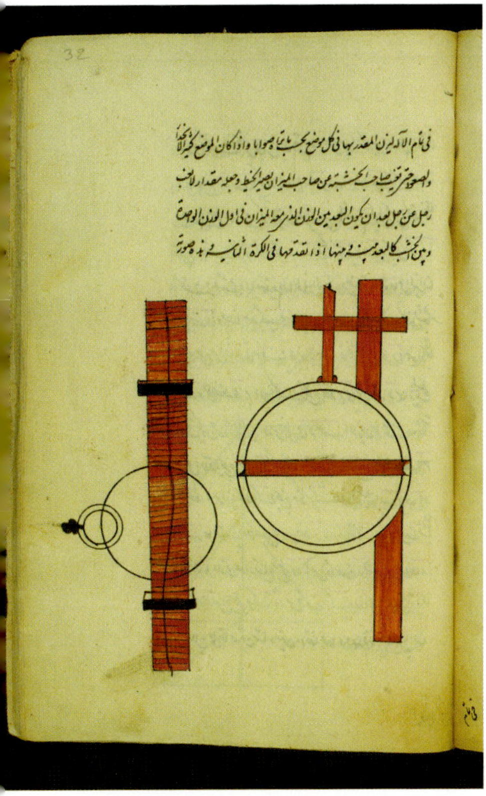

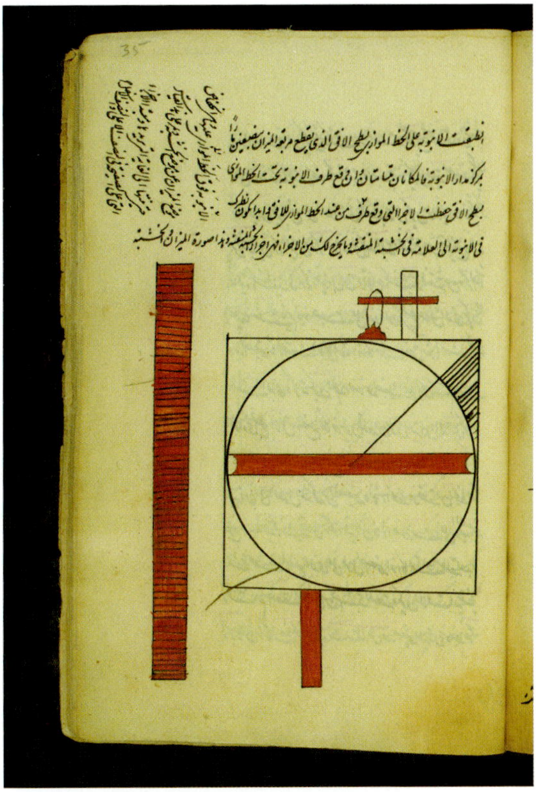

These two images are from al-Karaji's influential book on hydraulics and qanats. The book is regarded as one of his most useful contributions to the study of accessing freshwater.

means, according to Kowsar and Kowsar, "the mathematical concept of 'deduction by reasoning.'" They add, "These synonyms [*inbat* and *istenbat*] point to the vital importance of groundwater in a desert environment."

In this work, it is clear that al-Karaji possessed an extraordinary understanding of hydrology, which, simply put, is the study of the water on the earth. Water is the most important and vital component for human, plant, and animal life, but there is a limited amount of it. Water is found under the earth's surface, as well as in rivers, oceans, and other waterways. Hydrologists also study the water cycle. Also known as the hydrologic cycle, this is defined by the US Geological Survey as "a continuous process by which water is purified by evaporation and transported from the earth's surface (including the oceans) to the atmosphere and back to the land and oceans." Understanding the water cycle is essential because this is one of the ways in which the earth's water resources are replenished.

It is astounding to realize that al-Karaji had developed a sophisticated understanding of hydrology more than one thousand years ago. His book *The Extraction of Hidden Waters* is remarkable for its insights, and it must have been quite valuable to a culture that depended on finding and using water wisely. In an article, Danielle Bermudez cites Abigail Owen, a postdoctoral fellow at the University of Pittsburgh, who is working with a team to translate *The Extraction of Hidden Waters* into English. According to Bermudez, Owen "contends that al-Karaji's work should be celebrated as one of the oldest texts of its kind in the field of hydrology."

First of all, al-Karaji acknowledges the existence of a hydrological cycle and defines it in *The Extraction of Hidden Waters*. He writes: "The transformation of water into air in the hot regions and air into water in the cold regions creates a constant cycle which guarantees the prosperity of the lands."

Al-Karaji describes each part of this process: the way in which heat from the sun causes water to evaporate from the earth's surface, the way it is stored in clouds, and then the way in which rainwater falls back to the earth to replenish the lost moisture. He notes that much of this water seeps down beneath the earth's surface.

Interestingly, in the Quran, a passage refers to the ways in which God provided for the replenishment of the earth. The verse states, "We sent water in proper amounts from the skies and placed it in the earth." This may be a Quranic reference to groundwater, of which medieval Islamic scientists were aware. Al-Karaji refers to it as "hidden water" in his book. What exactly is groundwater?

Groundwater is water that is "hidden" or trapped between layers of rock beneath the earth's surface. There are layers of fragmented rock and soil underground, and the space between them can be filled with water. Those spaces are called aquifers. Water can flow through and around them. How does this water become trapped underground in the first place? Rainwater and melting snow can seep underground, through soil and dirt, and settle in the layers of rock.

In Karaj, the snow melting from the Elburz Mountains provided replenishment for the groundwater supply. In other words, the water, as al-Karaji realized, was there, and there was plenty of

The water cycle was little understood in al-Karaji's time. One of the main problems in the Middle East during this era was how to access freshwater and distribute it across the region, which is generally hot and dry.

Qanats are underground water tunnels. While this one, in the Yazd region, in modern-day Iran, is not used, many qanats are still functional and bring freshwater to villages and towns across the Middle East.

it. The question was, how could one access it and pull it out to be used by humans? One method that the ancient Persians developed were *qanats*, or water tunnels.

QANAT MASTER

In their important article on al-Karaji's studies of water extraction and the hydrological cycle, Kowsar and Kowsar declare that the medieval Islamic scholar was a "qanat master."

What are qanats? In Arabic, a qanat can be many different things, such as a waterway or a canal. In terms of al-Karaji's work, "qanats" referred to a vast system of underground water channels. They were built to collect water from a source, such as melting snows from a mountain range, and spread the precious resource underground through an intricate system of tunnels.

Al-Karaji may have perfected the construction of qanats, but he did not invent them. Qanats have a long history and demonstrate that the ancient Persians had worked for centuries to find ways to make dry land usable and inhabitable. The first qanats were built as early as 1,000 BCE in Persia. They were dug by hand, which took years of hard, grueling work that was often dangerous, as tunnels would collapse on workmen. However, the system was successful: a main tunnel would run from a source to the center of a village or town, and from there, it would branch out into several smaller tunnels that could be controlled through seals or gates. The tunnels could be opened to deliver water to homes or fields for irrigation or they could be sealed and the water would simply be stored underground for later use. In this way, the Persians were able to claim victory over the dry climate that threatened their survival—the qanats ensured access to water throughout the year.

How does the qanat system work? It works by using gravity to move water. As H. E. Wulff describes in *Scientific American*, a system of channels under the ground, qanats move water from aquifers in high lands to low levels using simple gravity. Like the great Roman acqueducts, Iran's qanats were built on a massive scale. Unlike the acqueducts of the Roman Empire, however, Iran's qanat works are still in use 3,000 years later! Iranians rely on the water they provide for both crop irrigation and household consumption. The qanats supply 75 percent of water used in Iran. And the system has expanded greatly. Iran has 22,000 qanat units that take up 170,000 miles (274,000 kilometers) of underground channels.

Indeed, when the Muslims conquered Persia and realized how effective the qanat system was, they began to construct them throughout the Islamic Empire. Eventually, qanats were built as far east as China and as far west as Spain!

How did al-Karaji, who was supposed to have retired, add to the already existing knowledge of qanats? His textbook offers important tips for the construction of these systems.

For example, he lists methods for detecting the presence of groundwater. "Snow was the surest source of water to Karaji," write Kowsar and Kowsar. Therefore, in the region of the Elburz Mountains, one way to know that an area is a reserve of underground water is to observe the mountains above it. If the

BUILDING A QANAT

In *Scientific American*, H. E. Wulff describes how a qanat was built in medieval Persia:

> On locating a promising spot, [the surveyor] arranges for the digging of a trial well.
>
> Two diggers, called muqanni, take up this task. They set up a windlass at the surface to haul up the excavated material in leather buckets and proceed to dig a vertical shaft about three feet in diameter, one man working with a mattock and the other with a short-handled spade.
>
> When they arrive at a moist stratum—a potential aquifer—the diggers scoop out a cavity to its impermeable clay bottom, and for the next few days the leather buckets are dipped into the hole periodically to measure the rate of accumulation of water in it. If more than a trickle of water is flowing into the hole, the surveyor can conclude that he has tapped a genuine aquifer. He may then decide to sink more shafts into the stratum in the immediate area to determine the extent of the aquifer and its yield.

The surveyor next proceeds to chart the prospective course of an underground conduit through which the water can flow from this head well or group of wells to the ground surface at some point farther down the slope ... For his measurements the surveyor uses simple instruments: a long rope and a level ... The surveyor lets the rope down to the water level in the well and marks the rope at the surface to show the depth ... As the muqanni proceed to dig the conduit itself, guide shafts are sunk to the indicated depths at intervals of about 300 yards to provide information regarding the route and pitch of the conduit for the diggers. They start the excavation of the conduit from the mouth end, digging into the alluvial fan. To protect the mouth from storm-water damage they often line the first 10 to 15 feet of the tunnel with reinforcing stone. The conduit is about three feet wide and five feet high. As the diggers advance they make sure they are following a straight course by sighting along a pair of burning oil lamps. They deposit the excavated material in buckets at the foot of the nearest ventilation shaft, and it is hauled up by their teammates above.

mountains are moist and black, this indicates that the snowfall there is plentiful and that the melted snow has been absorbed underground in the aquifers. Another method is to look for vegetation: the presence of plant life, which depends on water, indicates that water is present. "Flat-topped green, yellow and red mountains, consisting of layered rocks, occupied the second ranking in groundwater production" in al-Karaji's studies, Kowsar and Kowsar explain.

Furthermore, if one noted morning dew or morning fog in an area, then al-Karaji surmised that this meant groundwater was present. He even stated that another indicator was a "wail-like noise" that one could sometimes hear in the valleys of the mountainous region. The wail-like noise meant that there were empty pockets beneath the surface, underground, which were likely filled with water.

However, al-Karaji also offered a helpful list of plants that might indicate that water is not abundant. Such plants included camel thorn, which "amazed" al-Karaji, according to Kowsar and Kowsar: "He reported seeing one on the back of the Tigris River, which had been sent its root 15 zeraa [7.20 m]. He quoted a well-digger's report that had followed a camel thorn root to a 51 zeraa [24.48 m] deep water table."

These trees can grow in desert climates, as well as along riverbanks. They have adapted to their climate and they have the capacity to grow deep roots to seek water since water was not present in great quantities. They are tough trees that have resisted drought. Other such plants—which were indicators of a poor water supply—were black nightshade, wild hops, yellow sweet clover, licorice, and Arabian boxthorn. Instead, al-Karaji advised surveyors to look for areas where they could see plants that needed plentiful amounts of water for survival because that indicated that they were getting it.

CHAPTER FIVE

AL-KARAJI'S LEGACY

Like many of the greatest minds of his time, al-Karaji made important contributions across a wide range of fields. Today, scholars tend to become expert in one narrow field, but in al-Karaji's time, they studied a variety of subjects.

PROTECTING WORKERS

Al-Karaji also discussed the safety of qanat diggers and workmen in his book *The Extraction of Hidden Waters*. There were two hazardous facets of a qanat digger's job: the presence of gases in the tunnels, which suffocated the workers, and the fact that many tunnels often collapsed during construction because of soft soil.

Gases formed in qanats due to humidity in the tunnels, as well as the presence of dying plants. In his book, al-Karaji advised workers to avoid using kerosene to light their lamps as they worked in the dark tunnels. "Bee's wax and tallow from cattle, sheep, and pigs were preferred fuels," explain Kowsar and Kowsar. Interestingly, al-Karaji advised workers to avoid eating foods that caused flatulence, such as onions and garlic, before working, so that their gases would not add to the gases already in the tunnels!

He also devised ways to ventilate the tunnels so that diggers would benefit from supplies of fresh air as they worked. Qanat shafts should remain uncovered for a few days before work was conducted so that fresh air could penetrate the tunnel. Also, pipes made from leather could be pushed through the soil to connect the qanat to the surface and bring fresh air into the workspace.

The other major danger was the potential for qanats being constructed to collapse on the workers. Qanats were usually tiled to prevent water from leaking through and making the qanat weak and susceptible to a collapse. Al-Karaji suggested ways to improve the quality of the tiles that were used, as noted by Kowsar and Kowsar: "Karaji maintained that the tiles should be made of nonsaline earth lacking sand and should be well baked. Quicklime treated with olive oil, milk, or egg white made the best mortar for leak proofing the bell and spigot parts of the tiles."

Qanats are deep underground. This photograph depicts one of the "gates" of the qanat. Al-Karaji discovered ways to ventilate these tunnels to improve workers' safety conditions.

Many of al-Karaji's hydrological and extraction methodologies are still in wide use in Iran and other parts of the Middle East to this day. Researchers Pazwash and Mavrigian, in reflecting on *The Extraction of Hidden Waters*, are struck by how relevant al-Karaji's ideas are to the modern day: "Most significantly, the detailed accounts of descriptive theories and techniques regarding ground water are similar to descriptions found in present-day text-books."

H. E. Wulff agrees: "The methods used in Iran today are not greatly different from the system devised thousands of years ago." It was al-Karaji who consolidated and improved that system more than one thousand years ago.

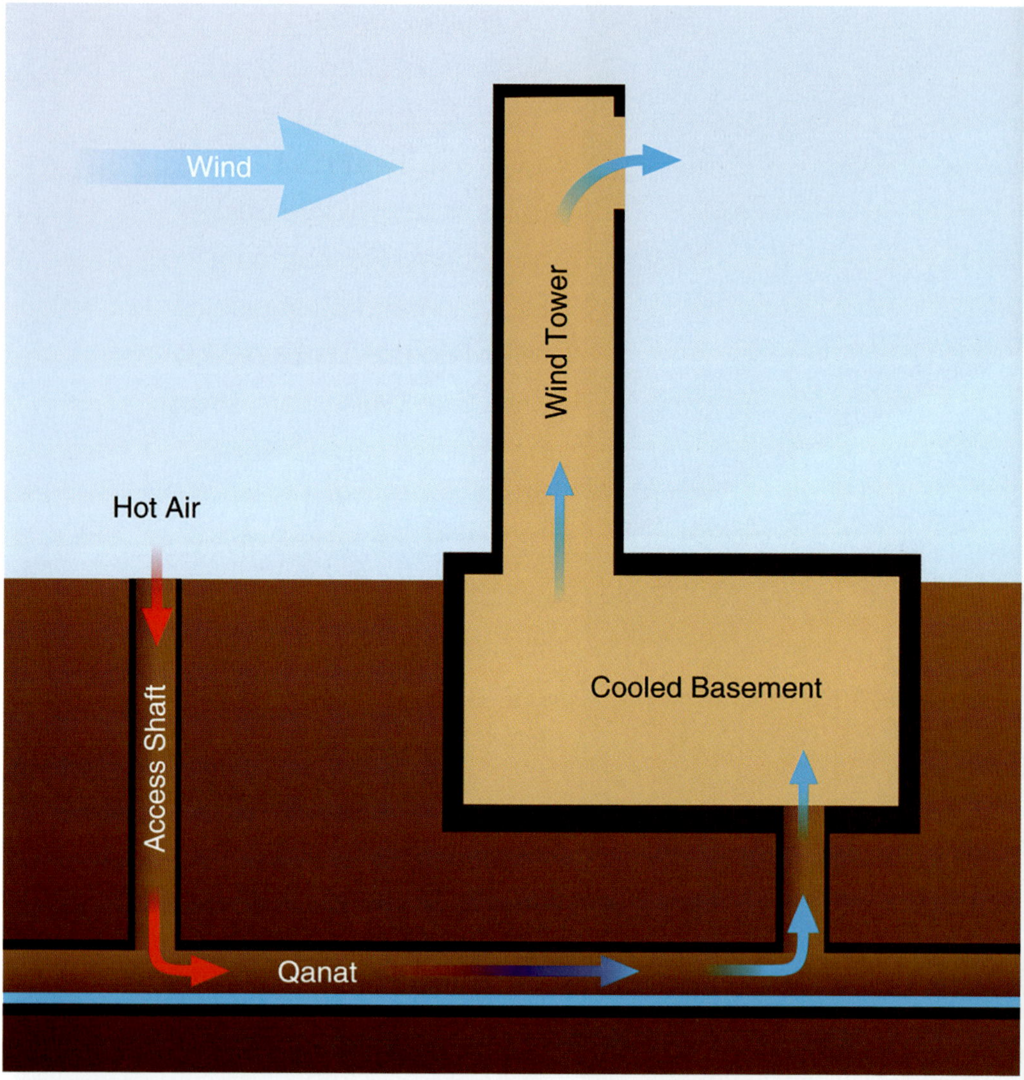

Qanats can be used to cool buildings. This diagram shows how the combination of the underground water stream and the air flow of a wind tower can achieve a cooling effect.

DEATH AND LEGACY

Muhammad al-Karaji died in either 1029 or 1030. Unfortunately, the exact date of his death is unknown, like many other aspects of his life. At the time of his death, he would have been approximately eighty years old, which was a long life by medieval standards.

There are questions that remain about his biography, including whether or not he married, whether or not he had children, and what contributions he made, if any, to other fields, such as astronomy. We know that he wrote a book about astronomy, but the manuscript has been lost. Historians have also wondered if he ever traveled beyond Baghdad and Persia.

There are also questions that persist about his legacy. One of the biggest overarching questions is this: was al-Karaji an original mathematician or someone who served as a transition between early works and modern algebra?

In order to answer that question, it is important to summarize what is known. For example, it is an indisputable fact that al-Karaji was an immensely gifted mathematician. He would never have been offered a position in the House of Wisdom, much less the position of a vizier, if he was not a talented mathematician. Furthermore, he was commissioned to write a textbook for civil servants on algebra and problem solving, and it is also possible that he established a school for teaching mathematics in Baghdad.

It is also clear that al-Karaji was prolific in his work. Historians believe that he wrote several more works and treatises that have been lost over time. As we know, some of his ideas were preserved only in the writings of mathematicians who succeeded him, such as al-Samawal. Other titles attributed to him, but whose full manuscripts are lost, include *Contracts and Buildings*, *The Book on Indian Mathematics*, *An Introduction to Astronomy*, and *The Book of Rare Theorems.*

In Iran, qanats are still popular sources of freshwater. Here, men work on a qanat, maintaining it and keeping it functioning. Many of al-Karaji's groundwater extraction methods are still used today.

An Arabic text depicting Pythagorus, one of the great mathematicians who helped devise theories in geometry. Muslim scholars worked hard to preserve and build on the work of previous mathematicians.

Al-Karaji also is responsible for making algebra an independent subject, free from the field of geometry and a separate field within mathematics. He defined and developed ideas that are still taught and used today, such as the binomial theorem and Pascal's triangle, as well as the addition, subtraction, and multiplication of polynomials.

In terms of hydrology and engineering, he wrote a manual on the detection and extraction of groundwater for human consumption and use that has only recently been recognized. According to Hormuz, "It is regrettable, due to the unfamiliarity of the western scholars to the Arabic language and Karaji's work that ethnographic descriptions and historical treatises on the subject of ground water totally neglected the name of Karaji as a scientific contributor. The significant fact is that the discovered printed works of Karaji appear now as the oldest treatise on ground water science. This manuscript hence proves to be a historical jewelpiece indeed."

It seems that, by examining this list of achievements, al-Karaji may safely be placed in the category of original scholars and thinkers, a person whose work advanced the knowledge at hand and made future scholarship possible.

RECOGNIZING AL-KARAJI

In 2012, Russian-born biologist Alexander J. Varshavsky was awarded the Prince Faisal International Prize for Science in Saudi Arabia. Varshavsky, who has held positions at the Massachusetts Institute of Technology and the National Institutes of Health, recognized al-Karaji's work in his acceptance speech. He said, "Modern science owes contributions by Arab scientists and physicians who lived and worked roughly a thousand years ago not too far from the place of today's magnificent ceremony. They contributed valuable insights to the world's civilization. The list of their achievements is very interesting and often startling." He named al-Karaji as one of these notable scholars of the past.

AL-KARAJI AND MODERN MATH AND SCIENCE

In 2010, Iran unveiled a new museum celebrating scientific achievements of Persians, and al-Karaji was one of four scientists whose work was featured. The museum was sponsored by the Iranian National Library and Archives, as well as the Iranian and Islamic

Civilization and Culture Committee. Al-Karaji's work is exhibited along with the accomplishments of Avicenna, the renowned Islamic philosopher and physician.

Al-Karaji's work continues to engage modern scientists. In *The Extraction of Hidden Waters*, he referred to a "blind, white fish that lives in the tunnels and is excellent for eating." This reference intrigued zoology student Anthony Smith, a student at Oxford University, so much so that he led an expedition of three fellow students to Persia to find the fish in 1950. He did not succeed, but the team's adventures in Persia were described in Smith's book *Blind White Fish in Persia*, which was published in 1952. Years later, Smith returned to try again, and this time he succeeded! Newspaper reports in 1976 proclaimed, "Legendary fish is for real." Smith had found a loach fish, related to the carp, that was indeed blind and that lived in the qanat tunnels. The scientific name given to the fish, *Noemacheilus smith*, recognizes his persistence in tracking down the fish, although it does not recognize the man who first described its existence—Muhammad al-Karaji.

Al-Karaji's books continue to fascinate modern mathematicians as well. In 2009, mathematicians from four continents—North America, South America,

Europe, and Australia—collaborated to try to solve a problem that al-Karaji had posed centuries ago. The problem related to right-angled triangles. According to the *Journal of Mathematics*, al-Karaji had originally asked, "For which whole numbers n does there exist a square a2 so that a2-n and a2+n are also squares?" The article explains, "When this happens, n is called a congruent number." It also noted that al-Karaji's problem, which had been unsolved for a thousand years, was similar in structure to problems posed by Diophantus, whose work al-Karaji admired.

Many mathematicians had attempted to solve the problem before, as early as Fibonacci in the 1200s.

Centuries ago, al-Karaji described the "blind white fish" who lived in qanats. The existence of that fish was confirmed only in the last century.

In 1952, mathematician Kurt Heegner made some advances, which were furthered by Jerrold Tunnell in 1982. But it was not until 2009 that an international team—Bill Hart (England), Gonzalo Tornaria (Uruguay), Mark Watkins (Australia), and Robert Bradshaw and David Harvey (United States)—found a solution.

In fact, they found 3,148,379,694 solutions. Using computers to help them in their calculations, they came up with more than three billion congruent numbers up to a trillion that worked!

It is possible that more of al-Karaji's work—and maybe more information about his life—will be discovered in the years to come and will continue to educate and engage mathematicians and scientists around the world.

TIMELINE

610 The prophet Muhammad begins to have visions of the angel Gabriel. He preaches to others on the Arabian Peninsula about the message of God.

622 Muhammad and his followers flee from Mecca to Medina and formally establish the Islamic faith.

633 The Persian Empire is conquered by the Muslims.

762 The Abbasid caliph Al-Mansoor begins plans to build a new capital on the banks of the Tigris River. It will be called Baghdad, or "given by god."

953 Abu Bakr ibn Muhammad ibn al-Husayn al-Karaji is born.

1010–1015 Al-Karaji is appointed to a government position, possibly that of a vizier, within the Abbasid administration in Baghdad.

c. 1015 Al-Karaji leaves Baghdad and retires to Persia.

1029 or 1030 Al-Karaji dies (it is believed) in Persia.

1130 Ibn Yahya al-Maghribi al-Samawal is born in Baghdad. A math prodigy, he will build upon many of al-Karaji's works and ideas.

1853 Franz Woepcke, a German mathematician, translates al-Karaji's book *Al-Fakhri* into French.

1879 Another German, Adolf Hochheim, translates al-Karaji's book *Sufficient on Calculation*.

1933 Giorgio Levi Della Vida argues that al-Karaji was Persian, not Arab.

1976 The existence of the "blind white fish" first described by al-Karaji is confirmed by scientists.

2009 An international team of mathematicians solves a math problem first posed by al-Karaji one thousand years prior.

2010 A new science museum in Iran features al-Karaji's work among the achievements of other Persian mathematicians and scientists.

GLOSSARY

algebra An order of mathematical thinking that manipulates symbols to represent and find the unknown.

algorithm A method or procedure for solving a problem. The term comes from the Latin translation of the name Al-Khwarizmi, a famous medieval Islamic mathematician.

aquifer Space filled with water that exists between layers of fragmented rock and soil underground.

binomial theorem A theorem that describes the expansion of powers of a binomial, or what happens when you multiply a binomial (a mathematical equation with two terms) by itself many times over.

caliphate A form of government in the medieval Islamic era in which the leader is the caliph, a successor to the prophet Muhammad.

coefficient A number or symbol multiplied with a variable in an algebraic term; for example, 4x means 4 multiplied by x (4 is the coefficient).

Crusades A series of military attacks by European Christian armies that attempted to overthrow the Islamic Empire in the Middle East, especially in Jerusalem, a city that is sacred to both Christians and Muslims.

determinate equations Math problems that have a solution.

geometry A branch of mathematics that studies shapes and their sizes, as well as their positions and properties.

groundwater Water supply that is "hidden," or trapped between layers of rock beneath the earth's surface.

Hadith A collection of the sayings and statements made by the prophet Muhammad during his lifetime, which Muslims believe offer instruction to Muslims for how to live a moral life.

hasib The Arabic word for a mathematician.

House of Wisdom An institute for learning and scholarship established in Baghdad by the Abbasid caliphate.

hydrology The study of water on Earth, including the water cycle.

indeterminate equations Math problems that have more than one solution.

Islam A monotheistic religion founded on the Arabian Peninsula by the prophet Muhammad in 622 CE.

mawalis Non-Arab Muslims, such as Persians, Turks, Kurds, and others, who had converted to Islam.

medieval Describing a time also known as the Middle Ages, the period of time from approximately 500 to 1500 CE.

monomial A mathematical expression that contains one ("mono-") term ("-nomial"); this means it can have a positive number and a coefficient or a variable.

monotheism A belief that there is only one ("mono-") deity. Judaism, Christianity, and Islam are all monotheistic religions.

Muslim A person who practices the faith of Islam.

Pascal's triangle The number pattern within a triangle that is formed by arithmetical calculations, by which a number within the triangle is always the sum of the two numbers above it.

patron A wealthy or powerful person who sponsors the studies or research of another.

polynomial A mathematical expression that contains "many" ("poly-") terms ("-nomial").

prolific The quality of having produced much work.

prophet In religious traditions, a knowledgeable person or teacher who conveys God's will to others.

qanats Water tunnels, first built by the Persians in 1000 BCE, to access groundwater.

Quran The sacred text of the Islamic faith, which Muslims believe was dictated to the prophet Muhammad by God through the angel Gabriel.

variable In mathematics, an unknown quantity represented by an alphabetic character, such as x or y.

zero From the Arabic word *sifir*, which means "empty," zero is an important concept developed by Indian mathematicians that allows the presence of "nothing" to be represented; it also helps in noting place value in numbers.

FOR MORE INFORMATION

American Mathematical Society (AMS)
201 Charles Street
Providence, RI 02904-2294
(800) 321-4267
Website: http://www.ams.org
AMS is a national organization dedicated to mathematical research and scholarship, as well as the promotion of careers in mathematics. It is the sponsor of the annual Who Wants to Be a Mathematician competition and many programs for students.

Association for Women in Mathematics (AWM)
11240 Waples Mill Road
Suite 200
Fairfax, VA 22030
(703) 934-0163
Website: https://sites.google.com/site/awmmath/home
This association was established in 1971 to promote mathematics as a career for women and girls. AWM has active student chapters as well as a national headquarters.

Canadian Mathematical Society
209 – 1725 St. Laurent Boulevard
Ottawa, ON K1G 3V4
Canada
(613) 733-2662, x785

Website: https://cms.math.ca
The society's goal is to "promote and advance the discovery, learning and application of mathematics." It holds annual meetings as well as math camps and other programs.

Institute of Islamic Studies
McGill University – Canada
Morrice Hall, Room 319
3485 McTavish Street
Montreal, QC H3A 0E1
(514) 398-6077
Website: https://www.mcgill.ca/islamicstudies/institute-islamic-studies
This academic institute focuses on the Islamic religion, history, and culture, as well as on current events in the Muslim world.

National Groundwater Association
601 Dempsey Road
Westerville, OH 43081
(800) 551-7379
Website: http://www.ngwa.org
This nonprofit association provides educational resources and guidance for the responsible use of and access to groundwater. Its website includes helpful resources for school-age students and teachers, including a Groundwater Adventurers program.

Technical Education Research Centers (TERC)
2067 Massachusetts Avenue
Cambridge, MA 02140
(617) 873-9600
Website: https://www.terc.edu/display/HOME/Home
Established in 1965, TERC has a simple mission: "to improve mathematics and science education." It works on various projects and programs to improve curricula in math and science and inspire students.

WEBSITES

Because of the changing nature of Internet links, Rosen Publishing has developed an online list of websites related to the subject of this book. This site is updated regularly. Please use this link to access the list:

http://www.rosenlinks.com/PSMI/karaji

FOR FURTHER READING

Ayduz, Salim, and Caner Dagli. *The Oxford Encyclopedia of Philosophy, Science, and Technology in Islam*. New York, NY: Oxford University Press, 2014.

Barnard, Bryn. *The Genius of Islam: How Muslims Made the Modern World*. New York, NY: Knopf: 2011.

Bramwell, Neil D. *Discover Ancient Persia*. New York, NY: Enslow, 2014.

Cohn, Jessica. *The Medieval Islamic World: Conflict and Conquest*. Huntington Beach, CA: Teacher Created Materials, 2013.

Cohn, Jessica. *Muhammad: Prophet of Islam*. Huntington Beach, CA: Teacher Created Materials, 2012.

Doak, Robin S. *Empire of the Islamic World*. New York, NY: Chelsea House Publishers, 2009.

Downey, Tika. *The History of Zero: Exploring Our Place-Value Number System*. New York, NY: Rosen Publishing, 2004.

Downey, Tika. *How the Arabs Invented Algebra: The History of the Concept of Variables*. New York, NY: Rosen Publishing, 2004.

Flatt, Lizann. *Early Islamic Empires*. New York, NY: Crabtree Publishing, 2011.

Friend, Robyn, and Judith Cohen. *Future Engineering: The Clean Water Challenge*. Marina del Rey, CA: Cascade Pass, 2015.

Guillain, Charlotte. *Islamic Culture*. Portsmouth, NH: Heinemann, 2014.

Habeeb, William Mark. *Iran*. Broomall, PA: Mason Crest, 2014.

Khalili, Jim al-. *The House of Wisdom: How Arabic Science Saved Ancient Knowledge and Gave Us the Renaissance.* New York, NY: Penguin: 2012.

Morgan, Michael H. *Lost History: The Enduring Legacy of Muslim Scientists, Thinkers, and Artists.* Washington, DC: National Geographic, 2008.

Nardo, Don. *The Islamic Empire.* Boston, MA: Greenhaven Press, 2011.

National Geographic. *1001 Inventions and Awesome Facts from Muslim Civilization.* Washington, DC: National Geographic, 2012.

Pickover, Clifford A. *The Math Book: From Pythagoras to the 57th Dimension, 250 Milestones in the History of Mathematics*. New York, NY: Sterling, 2012.

Rice, William. *Water Scientists: Earth and Space Science.* Huntington Beach, CA: Teacher Created Materials, 2007.

Romanek, Trudee. *Science, Medicine, and Math in the Early Islamic World*. New York, NY: Crabtree Publishers, 2012.

Samuels, Charlie. *Timeline of the Muslim World*. New York, NY: Gareth Stevens Publishing, 2010.

Strauss, Rochelle. *One Well: The Story of Water on Earth.* Toronto, Canada: Kids Can Press, 2007.

Taylor-Butler, Christine. *Hydrology: The Study of Water.* New York, NY: Scholastic, 2012.

Thompson, Bill, and Dorcas Thompson. *Iraq.* Broomall, PA: Mason Crest, 2014.

BIBLIOGRAPHY

American Institute of Mathematics. "Mathematicians Solve 'Trillion Triangle' Problem." Science News. ScienceDaily. September 22, 2009 (www.sciencedaily.com/releases/2009/09/090922095651.htm). Retrieved December 15, 2015.

Bermudez, Danielle. "Al-Karaji's Hidden Waters." Center for Humanities at UC Merced. November 3, 2015 (http://blogs.ucmerced.edu/centerforhumanities/2015/11/03/al-karajis-hidden-waters).

Bouaissa, Malikka. "The Crucial Role of Geometry in Islamic Art." Al.arte.magazine. July 27, 2013 (http://www.alartemag.be/en/en-art/the-crucial-role-of-geometry-in-islamic-art/).

Hill, Donald. *Islamic Science and Engineering*. Edinburgh, Scotland: Edinburgh University Press, 2003.

Kowsar, Sayyed Ahang, and Sayyedeh Shabahang Kowsar. "Karaji: Mathematician and Qanat Master." *Ground Water*, 50: 812–817, July 2012.

Los Angeles Times-Washington Post News Service. "Legendary Fish Is for Real." November 14, 1976 (https://news.google.com/newspapers?nid=861&dat=19761114&id=AENTAAAAIBAJ&sjid=kYUDAAAAIBAJ&pg=5580,2736558&hl=en).

McElroy, Tucker. *A to Z of Mathematicians*. New York, NY: Infobase Publishing, 2009.

O'Connor, J. J., and E. F. Robertson. "Abu Bekr ibn Muhammad ibn al-Husayn al_Karaji" (http://www-history.mcs.st-and.ac.uk/Biographies/Al-Karaji.html).

Pazwash, H., and G. Mavrigian. "A Historical Jewelpiece: Discovery of the Millennium Hydrological Works of Karaji." *JAWRA: Journal of the American Water Resources Association*, 1980, 16: 1094–1096.

Rashed, Roshdi. "Al-Karaji." *Dictionary of Scientific Biography*. 2008 (http://www.encyclopedia.com/doc/1G2-2830902256.html).

Saudi Aramco World. "Builder of Baghdad." November 1962 (http://archive.aramcoworld.com/issue/196209/builder.of.baghdad.htm).

Sessiano, Jacques. "Al-Karaji." *Encyclopaedia of the History of Science, Technology, and Medicine in Non-Western Cultures*. Edited by Helaine Selin. Berlin, Germany: Springer Science and Business Media, 2013.

Whittaker, Brian. "Centuries in the House of Wisdom." *Guardian*. September 22, 2004 (http://www.theguardian.com/education/2004/sep/23/research.highereducation1).

Wulff, H. E. "The Qanats of Iran." *Scientific American*. April 1, 1968 (http://www.scientificamerican.com/article/the-qanats-of-iran).

INDEX

A

Abbasids, 11, 20, 27, 28–29, 33, 34, 39, 40, 41, 42, 44, 46, 58, 62, 65, 68
Abu Bakr, 25
algebra, 12, 44, 50, 51, 55–56, 59, 87, 91
Ali, 25, 29
Arabs and Persians, differences between, 10–11, 30–31
Arithmetica, 44, 55, 56

B

Baghdad, 9, 11, 20, 29–33, 34, 41, 42, 54, 55, 59, 65, 87
base-10 number system, 45
Book of the Image of the Earth, The, 52
Brilliant on Algebra, 59

C

calligraphy, 8
Compendious Book on Calculation by Completion and Balancing, The, 49
Crusades, 15

D

Diophantus, 44, 55, 56, 58, 94

E

Elements, 44
Euclid, 44, 57, 58, 62
Extraction of Hidden Waters, The, 68–71, 82, 85, 93

G

geometry, 44, 62–63, 91
Glorious on Algebra, 11, 55, 56, 57
Golden Gate Palace, 33–34
groundwater, 71–73

H

Hadith, 6, 7, 34, 36
Hochheim, Adolf, 17–18
House of Wisdom, 34, 39, 46, 49, 54, 65, 87
hydrology/hydrological cycle, 70, 71, 75, 85, 91

I

Islam
  and education, 6, 9, 36–37, 40
  five pillars of, 6–7
  origins of, 20–23

K

Karaji, al-,

birthplace of, 10–11, 20
death of, 87
name of, 10–11, 16
works of, 11–12, 17, 18, 55, 56, 57–58, 62–63, 68–71, 82, 85, 88, 93
Khwarizmi, al-, 45, 46–54
influence on al-Karaji, 54–57
Khwarizmi Concerning the Hindu Art of Reckoning, Al-, 50

L

Levi Della Vida, Giorgio, 18–20

M

Mamun ibn Haroun, al–, 46, 49
Mansoor, Jafar Abdallah al–, 29
Martel, Charles, 26–27
Muawiyah ibn Abi Sufyan, 26
Muhammad, the prophet, 6, 7, 20–23, 25, 28, 34, 36, 37
Mulk, Fakhr al-, 55, 65

P

paper, invention of, 40–41
Pascal, Blaise, 61
Pascal's triangle, 60–61, 91
Persians and Arabs, differences between, 10–11, 30–31

Q

qanats, 75–77, 78–79, 82–83
Quran, 6, 7, 8, 9, 21, 34, 36, 37, 40, 71

R

Rashid, Haroun al-, 46
Rashidun, 25

S

Samawal, Ibn Yahya al-Maghribi al–, 58–60
Smith, Anthony, 93
Sufficient on Calculation, 12, 18, 62, 63

T

Tours, Battle of, 26

U

Umar, 25
Umayyads, 26–27, 29, 42
Uthman, 25

W

Woepcke, Franz, 12, 17, 55
Wonderful on Calculation, 11, 57–58

Z

zero, concept of, 45, 50, 52
Zoroastrianism, 30–31

ABOUT THE AUTHOR

Susan Nichols has written several young adult biographies and nonfiction books. She teaches English literature and writing, and lives in Baltimore, Maryland, with her family.

PHOTO CREDITS

Cover. p. 69 Lawrence J. Schoenberg Collection of Manuscripts, Kislak Center for Special Collections, Rare Books and Manuscripts, University of Pennsylvania; cover (background), pp. 3, 16, 30, 31, 36, 37, 51, 78, 79, 92 gfxmart/Shutterstock.com; p. 5 Iqbal Khatri/Moment/Getty Images; pp. 6-7 kickimages/E/Getty Images; pp. 12-13 Institute of Oriental Studies, St. Petersburg, Russia/Bridgeman Images; pp. 14-15 Leemage/Universal Images Group/Getty Images; pp. 18-19 Adwo/Shutterstock.com; pp. 22-23 De Agostini Picture Library/Getty Images; p. 24 Courtesy of the University of Texas Libraries, The University of Texas at Austin; p. 27 Photo © Tallandier/Bridgeman Images; p. 32 © British Library Board/Robana/Art Resource, NY; p. 33 Gianni Dagli Orti/The Art Archive at Art Resource, NY; p. 35 Print Collector/Hulton Archive/Getty Images; p. 38 bpk, Berlin/Bibliotheque Nationale, Paris, France/Art Resource, NY; pp. 42-43 Edinburgh University Library, Scotland/With kind permission of the University of Edinburgh/Bridgeman Images; p. 47 Eduard Kim/Shutterstock.com; pp. 48-49 San Diego Museum of Art, USA/Edwin Binney 3rd Collection/Bridgeman Images; pp. 52-53 Encyclopaedia Britannica/Universal Images Group/Getty Images; p. 61 SPL/Science Source; p. 64 De Agostini/C. Sappa/Getty Images; pp. 66-67 oxine/Shutterstock.com; pp. 72-73 wawritto/Shutterstock.com; pp. 74-75 Ilia Torlin/Shutterstock.com; pp. 84-85 Naeinsun/Wikimedia/File:Rigareh second gate edited.jpg/CC BY-SA 3.0; p. 86 Samuel Bailey/Wikimedia/File:Qanat wind tower.svg/CC BY 3.0; pp. 88-89 Georg Gerster/Science Source; p. 90 Oesterreichische Nationalbibliothek, Vienna, Austria/Archives Charmet/Bridgeman Images; pp. 94-95 imageBROKER/SuperStock

Designer: Michael Moy; Editor: Christine Poolos;
Photo Researcher: Nicole DiMella